MANTOR MENACE

TM and © BVS Entertainment, Inc. and BVS International N.V. All rights reserved.
Adapted by Slade Stone from the original scripts by Bruce Kalish and Jackie Marchand
Illustrated by Scott Neely and William Phillips

08 09 10 11   B&M 10 9 8 7 6 5 4 3 2 1
17425 Power Rangers 8x8 - Jungle Fury: Mantor Menace

Ten thousand years ago there was a great evil in the world named Dai Shi. He believed that animals should rule the planet and humans were to be erased. Brave warriors channeled their animal spirits and, after a great battle, captured Dai Shi and imprisoned him in a locked box. This box has been guarded by the secretive kung fu clan, the Pai Zhuq—Order of the Claw.

One young and talented student at the kung fu school has foolishly unleashed his own rage—knocking the box from the master's hands. The dark spirit of Dai Shi escapes the box, laughing out, "Free! Free-e-e-e-e!"

Three brave teens are selected from all the students at the kung fu school to seek out and destroy Dai Shi. These are the Jungle Fury Power Rangers, trained well, but with much yet to learn.

Casey, the Red Ranger, is an excellent and strong fighter, but he has never liked rules. He is willing to take risks—but he resists the discipline of practice. When he needs to boost his attack power, he calls forth his animal spirit—the Red Tiger.

Theo, the Blue Ranger, follows all the rules, but his "by the book" approach turns to "by the claw" action when evil is confronted. Like his animal spirit, the Blue Jaguar, he is smart and quick!

Lily, the Yellow Ranger, has a heart of gold. She tends to plays it cool—just like her animal spirit, the Yellow Cheetah. She uses her fined-tuned hip-hop dance moves to sidestep attacks and surprise the enemy.

High on a mountaintop near the coastal town of Ocean Bluff, the evil Dai Shi rules in his temple. He commands:

"Too long have you rested, waiting for this day. Arise, my army of fear! Arise, my Rin Shi!"
From the cracks in the floor, dark energy seeps out and forms a growling, hissing army of Rin Shi soldiers.

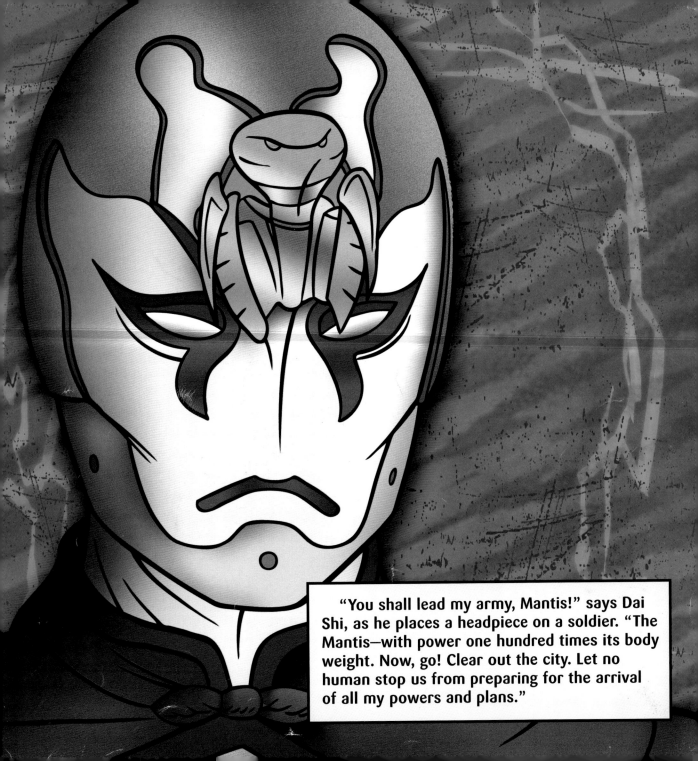

"You shall lead my army, Mantis!" says Dai Shi, as he places a headpiece on a soldier. "The Mantis—with power one hundred times its body weight. Now, go! Clear out the city. Let no human stop us from preparing for the arrival of all my powers and plans."

The Rin Shi's attack on the city is devastating. As the people run in terror, the Rin Shi grow stronger, gaining energy from the fear. Rin Shi Mantis grows more powerful with every scream—finally transforming into the monstrous Mantor!

"Now for some real destruction!" he roars. "When I break the city dam, it will flood Ocean Bluff! It will clear everything away for the arrival."

The three teens grab their Solar Morphers and go into action. Together they call out:

"Jungle Beast, Spirit Unleashed!"

The sunglasses transform them into an unbeatable trio.
"With the strength of a Tiger!" calls Casey. "Jungle Fury Red Ranger!"
"With the speed of a Cheetah!" calls Lily. "Jungle Fury Yellow Ranger!"
"With the stealth of a Jaguar!" calls Theo. "Jungle Fury Blue Ranger!"
"We summon the animal spirits from within. Power Rangers, Jungle Fury!"

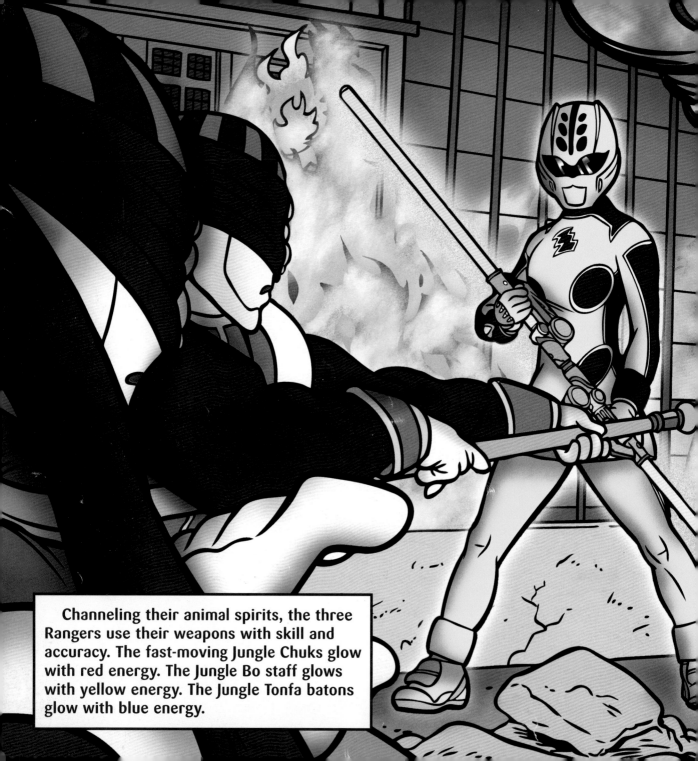

Channeling their animal spirits, the three Rangers use their weapons with skill and accuracy. The fast-moving Jungle Chuks glow with red energy. The Jungle Bo staff glows with yellow energy. The Jungle Tonfa batons glow with blue energy.

Casey, the Red Ranger, spins to face Mantor. "Hey, bug breath, you're next!"

"You are mere insect pests to me," Mantor scoffs as he grows in size and flings powerful discs out of his claws, which hit the dam. The concrete begins to crack!

"Things are about to get wet and wild!" calls Casey as a torrent of water heads through the streets. "It's time to combine our animal spirits!"

"Three spirits—work as one!" call the three Rangers. "Jungle Fury Power Rangers!"
The three cat spirits leap into the air and become great machine Zords, with the
Rangers at the controls. They pounce on Mantor, knocking him to the ground.
But, amazingly, Mantor recovers—and continues to grow!

"Whoa!" yells Lily.
"Giant mantis alert."
"It's combo time, cats!"
cries Casey.
With the call of
JUNGLE PRIDE MEGAZORD...

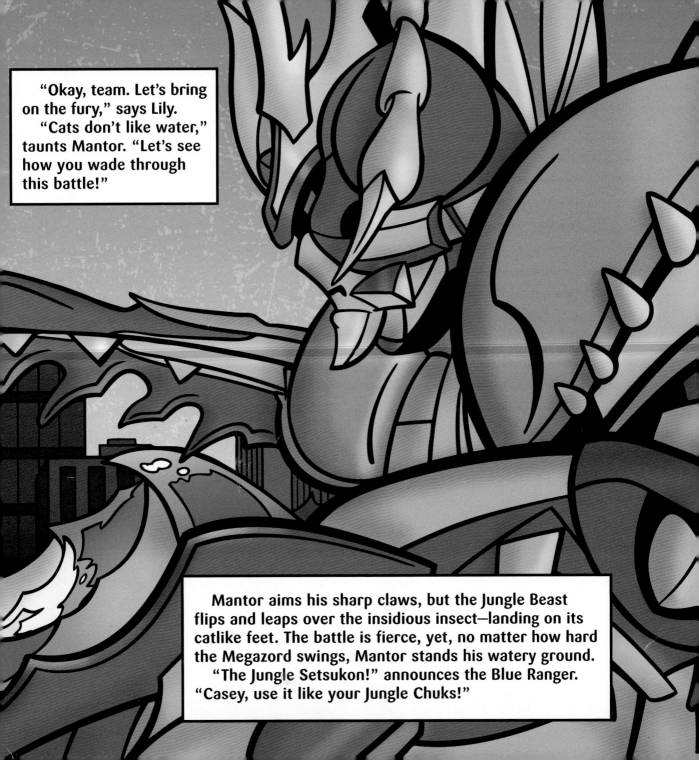

"Okay, team. Let's bring on the fury," says Lily.

"Cats don't like water," taunts Mantor. "Let's see how you wade through this battle!"

Mantor aims his sharp claws, but the Jungle Beast flips and leaps over the insidious insect—landing on its catlike feet. The battle is fierce, yet, no matter how hard the Megazord swings, Mantor stands his watery ground.

"The Jungle Setsukon!" announces the Blue Ranger. "Casey, use it like your Jungle Chuks!"

"All over it!" the Red Ranger calls back.

The weapons combine to form the ultimate kung fu weapon.

"Oh... no!" moans Mantor. "Not the..."

"Savage Spin!" call the Rangers.

The arms of the Megazord spin with awesome power and hit the mighty menace with incredible force. The monster turns to stone, crumbles—and explodes!

"Yes!" cheers Lily. "That pest is exterminated!"
That's what happens when you fight with your brains," says Theo.
"And your heart," adds Lily.
"And your strength!" declares Casey. "Next time, Dai Shi better
send more than a bug to match the power of us cool cats!"